Dear Readers,

We're so excited about our new book series, Sprouse Bros. 47 R.O.N.I.N.! When we decided to develop a book series, we wanted to create stories kids our age would love. So we jam-packed our series with all of the cool things we love to read about—top secret plots, ninja fighters, ancient samurai weapons, and ultimate villains. We even have a lot in common with the main characters, Tom and Mitch, from our favorite desserts to our favorite bands. Because we love comics so much, we've included original comic book–style art—illustrated by an awesome comic book artist—in each book. We think it rocks, and we hope you do too!

Thanks for reading our series, and stay tuned for future episodes of Sprouse Bros. 47 R.O.N.I.N.!

Dylan Sprouse and Cole Sprouse

We would like to thank our dad,
Matt, and our manager, Josh, for
their constant support. Thanks also
to everyone at Dualstar and Simon &
Schuster for all of their hard work.
Last, but not least, thanks to all of our
friends and fans—this is for you guys!
—Dylan Sprouse and Cole Sprouse

Marc Cerasini wishes to thank
Alice Alfonsi for her invaluable
help with the preparation of
this manuscript.

This book is a work of fiction. Any references to historical events, real people, or real locales are used fictitiously. Other names, characters, places, and incidents are the product of the author's imagination, and any resemblance to actual events or locales or persons, living or dead, is entirely coincidental.

SIMON SPOTLIGHT
An imprint of Simon & Schuster Children's Publishing Division • 1230 Avenue of the Americas, New York, New York 10020
Sprouse Bros.™ and related Sprouse Bros. trademarks are trademarks of DC Sprouse Inc., and licensed exclusively by Dualstar Entertainment Group, LLC. © 2007. DC Sprouse, Inc. All rights reserved. • All rights reserved, including the right of reproduction in whole or in part in any form.
SIMON SPOTLIGHT and colophon are registered trademarks of Simon & Schuster, Inc.
Manufactured in the United States of America • 10 9 8 7 6 5 4 3 2
ISBN-13: 978-1-4169-3903-0 • ISBN-10: 1-4169-3903-2
Library of Congress Catalog Card Number 2007926906

SPROUSE bros

47 r·o·n·i·n

EPISODE 4 THE SIEGE

by Marc Cerasini
with Dylan Sprouse and Cole Sprouse
based on the series concept created by Marc Cerasini
with Dylan Sprouse and Cole Sprouse
interior illustrations by Lawrence Christmas
insert illustrations by Dan Panosian

Simon Spotlight
New York London Toronto Sydney

The superior man is firm in the right way,
and not merely firm.
—Confucius

CHAPTER 1

BRIDGE OF THE SHIP RAKURAI, PACIFIC OCEAN

"We're going to *this* island." Mitch Hearn pointed at the frayed map. His index finger tapped a tiny land mass with a longitude between the Philippine Sea and the international date line.

"Weird," mumbled his brother Tom.

"What?" said Mitch. "Is something wrong with the coordinates?"

"No."

Mitch scratched his shaggy blond head. "Then what's so *weird* about the island?"

"Nothing." Tom folded his arms. His biceps looked more pumped than usual since he'd just finished a workout on the glass-enclosed deck. "I wasn't referring to the island."

"Then what were you—"

"It's weird to see you using a paper map, that's all,"

said Tom. "You're usually glued to a GPS screen."

"He's got a point, Mitch." Brian Saito laughed, his round cheeks flushing. "A paper map on a ship like this is like, I don't know. It's like—"

"A buggy whip on a Ferrari," Tom finished.

Mitch couldn't argue with that. After all, the *Rakurai* was the most technically advanced ship he'd ever seen, let alone been on. Everything on the *Rakurai* was fully automated, from the hydrofoil wings made from top secret composite materials, to the dual-turbine, solar-powered engines.

That was one reason he was glad Brian had asked to come with them on this journey.

Tom was good with computers, but Brian was a genius, and the bridge they now stood on probably had as many servers as the Matsu School's mainframe.

Despite the ship's phenomenal capabilities, however, Mitch knew that all the digital maps in the *Rakurai*'s vast archives couldn't help them—only this old, wrinkled chart could.

"Yeah, but this map is the only one that can help us find what we're looking for," Mitch reminded everyone.

The map they were using was the one Mr. Chance had found in Dr. Gensai's lab, after he and his daughter were kidnapped. Emiko Gensai had been their classmate at the Matsu School, an elite computer science academy run by the Matsu Cybernetics Corporation. After she'd been snatched off the Tokyo streets one night, Mitch and Tom had begun following clues to find her.

Although they had yet to locate Emiko or her father, they'd uncovered evidence that Julian Vane was involved in their disappearance, along with his Black Lotus gang, a group of savage ninja warriors who were the mortal enemies of R.O.N.I.N. This wasn't so surprising, as Julian Vane seemed to be behind the disappearances of many others, including Inoshiro Matsu, as well as Laura's father, Mr. Ting—and most importantly, Tom and Mitch's father, Jack Hearn.

After learning of Emiko's kidnapping, Nikki Matsu had lent Tom and Mitch her company's cutting-edge ship so they could track Vane down and hopefully rescue some of the people he had captured.

Mitch and his "crew" had sailed out of Tokyo Bay at sunset and quickly shifted the *Rakurai* into superfast hydrofoil mode. The sleek ship's submerged wings came to the surface. The hull and glass-enclosed decks above it rose out of the water, reducing the drag enormously. Then the three-hundred-ton, two-hundred-foot-long ship started traveling at full power, rocketing over the water with the smoothness of a seabird.

After several hours, the sky changed from deep purple to pitch black—save for the million points of starlight scattered across the vast dark bowl above them. Dinner was cooked and served by Mr. Chance. Then he brought tea up to the bridge before retiring for the night.

Now it was late, and Mitch was tired too. He could see that Tom, Brian, and Laura Ting were looking pretty beat, but he'd called this crew meeting anyway, just to make sure everyone was on the same page—*his* page.

"As you can see," Mitch continued, "Dr. Gensai marked the location of his first stop in ink, with the exact longitude and latitude scribbled next to his mark."

"Yeah, okay," said Tom, shoving his hands into the pockets of his jeans. "But how do you know this is Dragon Island?"

"I don't," Mitch replied. "It's more likely that it *isn't* Dragon Island, but it's a place to start."

"Why?" asked Tom. "Why would we go to this island if it isn't the right place?"

"Because it's our only clue right now," said Mitch. "Maybe we'll find *another* clue when we get there."

Tom snorted. "We should be tracking down Julian Vane instead, forcing him to tell us Dragon Island's location, not to mention his plans for everyone else he's captured."

Back in Tokyo, Mitch and Tom had already stopped one of Vane's deadly schemes. But they suspected that the man had another, even bigger one in the works. Emiko and her dad seemed to be the key to making this next plot happen; otherwise, Vane never would have risked snatching them.

Julian Vane usually did things carefully. He was a strategist. That's how the man had become a billionaire in the first place. He'd been born with money, but nothing close to the fortune he had now. He'd plundered it over the years, like a financial pirate.

In Mitch's view, the choice of tactics was vital in winning an argument like this. And although it was typical of Tom to want to confront Vane directly, it would not get them any closer to Dragon Island.

Mitch knew it would take smart moves to checkmate Julian Vane, and he was more than up for the game. He preferred a more methodical strategy, intending to gather data, do analysis, and draw up a response to Vane that relied heavily on the element of surprise.

To stop the man, they'd have to stop his plan. And to Mitch that meant unraveling Vane's scheme bit by bit, using logic and patience.

"Sorry, Pokey," Mitch told his brother, "Mr. Chance didn't appoint *you* the acting captain. He appointed me."

Mitch could hear how harsh and condescending his tone was getting, but he just couldn't help himself.

Tom shook his head. "Listen, Motormouth, Mr. Chance only appointed you acting captain because this tub's nothing more than a floating IT room."

"So what if it is?" Mitch snapped back. "I've already punched the coordinates into the ship's navigational program. We're already en route, end of discussion."

"End of discussion?" Tom's eyes narrowed. "Listen, bro, I know you think you can't *ever* be wrong, but your 'strategy' has more holes than a doughnut shop—"

"You're wrong," interrupted Mitch. "The dates and general coordinates of Dr. Gensai's last voyage are all on his handwritten notes. One of them could be the island you've been seeing in your dreams—"

"*Could* be," said Tom. "That's hole number one."

"There's no getting around the fact that a lot of what's marked here is unknown," Mitch argued.

"Hole number two: the unknown," Tom countered. "You have no idea what's on those islands. We could be sailing into a pile of trouble—"

"Or not," Mitch cut in. "That's *why* we have to investigate. Any description beyond the coordinates is locked inside Gensai's laptop computer—"

"Which is still fried," said Laura. She'd been silent during the entire meeting. Now she spoke up. "It *is* still fried, isn't it?" she asked, looking at Mitch.

"I'm still working on it," Mitch said defensively. He

folded his arms across his chest and frowned.

"It's okay," Laura said, suppressing a yawn. She tossed back her long black ponytail and shoved her hands into the front pocket of her oversize hoodie. "I'm not giving you a hard time. I was just hoping maybe you had more luck than I did."

"Why should he?" Tom questioned. "You tried to restore the computer and you failed. And you're at least as good as he is when it comes to microchips. It might be impossible to fix."

"Well, as the captain of this ship"—Mitch pounded a fist into his palm—"I say nothing is impossible!"

Tom rolled his eyes. "A few hours sitting in a captain's chair and he thinks he's Captain Kirk."

"He's not a bad role model, you know," Mitch countered. "He's an excellent Starfleet officer."

Tom threw up his hands. "He's fictional!"

"I don't care what you say." Mitch resolutely folded his arms. "My plan is the way to go about finding what we're looking for."

Tom groaned and pointed to Gensai's dead laptop. "Then you better get back to work unfrying that computer, Motormouth, 'cause your 'plan' seems to have a lot in common with wishful thinking."

"Chill, Tom," Brian interrupted, putting a hand on his shoulder. "Mitch's plan is just standard operating

procedure. You learn a lot about this stuff traveling the world as an army brat. Before my dad gets into his navy jet, SOP in carrier mechanics dictates that he check every system before launching it. We're simply going to visit every island that Dr. Gensai visited, one by one, and check them off our list. What's the harm in being methodical?"

Tom brushed Brian's hand away. "The harm is that it wastes time."

"Ignore my brother," Mitch told Brian, waving dismissively. "He has a big problem with patience."

"What?" Tom reeled on Mitch. "*I* have a big problem with patience? Maybe if *you* were the one having nightmares about Dragon Island and some endangered scroll, you'd feel differently about *wasting time*!"

Mitch gritted his teeth.

"Listen to me, Tom, unless you want to hit the sack and dream us a map with a direct route, we're going to do what I say because *I'm* the captain!"

"Oh, yes, sir!" Tom shot his brother a mock salute, then wheeled and stalked off in disgust.

"Come back here!" Mitch commanded. "This meeting is not over until I say it is!"

But Tom was already gone. Laura exchanged an embarrassed glance with Brian. Neither of them wanted to get in the middle of the feuding brothers. "I guess I'll go back to my cabin too," she said quietly.

"Yeah . . . ," Brian agreed, feigning a yawn. "We're all just really tired. We can pick this up in the morning, after we all cool off, right, Captain?"

Mitch did not reply. With the ship's motor quietly purring in the background, he stared out the window at the murky ocean waves until he was alone on the bridge. Then he returned to the old map, unfolding it completely.

Dr. Gensai's wrinkled chart was so big it covered most of the control panel. For the first time, Mitch noticed a scribbled note in the corner. The words were in English, but very small, and the writing was sloppy.

Mitch pulled out a magnifying glass to get a better look. When he made out the words, his eyes widened and he gasped.

"Beware of pirates!" the passage warned.

CHAPTER 2

"I'm flying again," Tom murmured. Strong gales whipped his hair and face. Salty air filled his nostrils; the scent of ocean was overpowering! Only then did he notice there was no paragliding harness around him. Tom was flying like a gull on the wind.

He loved being in the middle of the sky, with the dark ocean roiling below him . . . until he realized he was quickly headed downward. Suddenly he was no longer in control of his flight. Instead, he was plummeting rapidly. The rocky landscape rose up to meet him. Tom closed his eyes, waiting for the impact. But it never came.

When he opened his eyes, all he could see was the burning of two emerald green lights off in the distance. This time he knew they weren't lanterns. They were the eyes of the majestic jade dragon, wingless, fierce yet tranquil, standing like a sentry at the top of an island mountain.

Tom knew this place, too. It was Dragon Island, the

secret R.O.N.I.N. sanctuary. He'd been here many times before, in his dreams. Now, he was back.

Suddenly helicopters appeared. They circled the mountaintop. Men in black battlesuits jumped from the choppers and burst into the cave. Seconds later, Tom saw the flash of gunfire.

"We must protect the Scroll!" called a deep voice. Tom saw the dragon statue move. Its emerald eyes glowed brighter as it spoke again. "Protect the Scroll at all costs."

Suddenly Tom found himself inside the cave. An old man in a green robe rushed forward. Tom knew this man too from his earlier dreams. He was the leader of R.O.N.I.N. He was the Dragon—and the voice in Tom's dreams.

"Wait!" Tom called out.

But the Dragon couldn't hear him. Tom watched him grab a large, ornate scroll from its hiding place and then dash into the darkness of the cave. A half-dozen black suits chased him, then all of them were swallowed up by the dark. Tom knew this would happen. He had seen it happen before.

Like a soaring spirit, Tom followed them through the pitch-black mountain, penetrating the centuries of rock and dirt with ease. But this was where his previous dream had ended.

Please let me figure something out, Tom pleaded. I

have to keep dreaming. . . . I just have to.

As if in answer to his prayer, Tom continued to follow the man in the green robe. The rest of the suits seemed to have faded away. Eventually, the Dragon came to a small, rocky chamber, and Tom watched as he walked into the chamber, toward two shadowy figures, with the scroll clutched tightly in his hands. Tom had never seen these two small figures in his dreams before. Who were they? The old man steered them toward a nook hidden within the chamber, and handed the scroll to one of them.

"You must protect the scroll," he ordered, although in a fatherly voice. "Do not let it out of your sight. If someone finds you, scream as loud as your voices will carry and then run as far away as you can. Can you do this?"

The figures nodded their heads in silent obedience.

"Hey, who are they? What's happening?" He called out to the Dragon and the two figures. But no one could hear him. It was as if he were invisible.

Then suddenly, the Dragon stepped away and dashed back out through the entrance of the chamber. Tom followed him at once, desperate for answers. He trailed him back through the cold, dank passageways for what seemed like miles. Tom tripped more than once over the rocky walkway, but not one of his falls alerted the old man to his presence. Then he heard the shuffling of feet, and the cocking of weapons grew noisier. They were again near the main room where the attackers would be waiting.

The old man scurried behind the wall to assess his attackers. The room was surrounded by at least fifty men in black battlesuits, all with their heads covered. The man knew he was defeated; it was over.

As he stepped out of the shadows, the Dragon asked in a calm yet stern voice, "What do you want?"

"You know what we are here for, old one. Where is it?" growled a raspy voice. Tom stepped out into the archway of the main room to catch a glimpse of who was speaking. Whoever he was, he had to be extremely powerful to arrange an attack this elaborate.

"At least show me your face, before you rob me of my most valuable possession," the Dragon said. "I believe it is my right to know who my attacker is."

"You have no rights as far as I am concerned," the voice replied. "But take me to the scroll and I will oblige, because I want you to know who I am so you can remember how powerful I am. And bring me the two newest R.O.N.I.N. members. Yes, yes, of course I know they are here. Do not defy me; I shall simply take them by force if I must."

Looking weary and scared, the old man sighed heavily

as he realized he had no choice; he was surrounded. Tom could feel all hope escape from him.

"I shall do so without fail or resistance if you promise me you will not harm them," the Dragon told his opponent. "They are innocent, and know nothing of what goes on here, or the contents of the scroll. Please, I beg you, let them return home."

"It seems to be your lucky day, old man, as once again, your wish will be granted. They will remain unharmed, but not on your orders. They are far too valuable to dispose of . . . yet. Now take me to them."

The Dragon shuffled back through the entrance of the main room and into the maze that would bring them to the smaller, rocky chamber. The goon and three of his men followed them, and Tom walked briskly amongst them all. When they entered, the old man approached the small nook and kneeled down.

"I'm afraid we have been defeated, young ones," he said. "But do not fear, you will not be harmed. Please, hand me the scroll."

One of the figures shifted inside the nook and extended a small hand, which was gripping the scroll tightly. Tom tried to get closer to them, to see who they were. The Dragon called them "young ones." How young could they be? How had they come to be on the island? Were they really going home, or were they in danger?

"Here," the old man announced, handing the scroll to the man in black. "You have what you came for. I am a man of my word. Are you?"

The man in black began to laugh, and then slowly lifted the mask off his face. Tom's jaw dropped, and he screamed. He couldn't believe his eyes, yet there was no doubt in his mind that he was staring at . . . Julian Vane.

"Land ho!"

Tom woke to a blinding light. His cabin was awash in the glaring rays of a rising sun. It shone through the large porthole.

He threw a hand over his eyes and groaned. Oh, man, he thought. Why didn't I close the curtains before I went to sleep?

Lying perfectly still, Tom took a deep breath and tried to call back the last bit of his fuzzy dream/vision.

"Julian Vane?" he murmured, rubbing his eyes. "I saw Julian Vane on Dragon Island. . . ." He sighed and slowly sat up in his bunk. "And who are the two young ones?"

"Land ho!"

For the second time, Tom heard the dopey call. It sounded like the overexcited voice of Brian Saito.

Bang! Bang! Bang! Tom's cabin door flew open. "Wake up, sleeping beauty," Mitch called, glancing at his watch. "We've reached our first checkpoint!"

"Checkpoint?" Tom yawned and rubbed his eyes again.

"Dr. Gensai's first island! Get a move on, Pokey!" Mitch commanded, and then he disappeared, leaving the door wide open.

Tom sighed and swung his bare legs off the edge of his bunk. Squinting against the glare, he peered out the porthole at the three-mile stretch of land, sitting amid the vast blue-green ocean. The small puddle of earth was flat as a pancake and covered by a dense carpet of trees. No majestic mountain. No jade dragon.

"Great," Tom mumbled. "Our first wasted stop."

"What did you say, Tom?"

Tom wheeled to find Laura Ting passing by his open door. Gone were the oversize hoodie and camouflage pants of the night before. Today she was wearing neon pink shorts and a fitted white tank. Her long hair was loose from its usual ponytail and a little bit damp, like she'd just gotten out of the shower.

"Whoa!" said Tom in surprise.

She paused in the doorway, staring blankly at Tom in his pajamas. Embarrassed, he grabbed his jeans off the back of a chair and draped them in front of him.

"C'mon, Laura, I'm not dressed here!"

Laura folded her arms and leaned against the

doorjamb. "Do you know how many brothers I grew up with back in Chinatown?" She smiled. "I've seen pajamas before, you know. Yours aren't anything special."

"Well, I'm not one of your brothers!" Tom exclaimed. His face and forehead suddenly felt hot. *If I'm blushing right now, she'll never let me forget it. This is seriously embarrassing.*

"You want to spar with me later?" Laura asked. "I haven't had a decent workout since we fought those Yakuzas back at Mount Fuji. And Mitch says he's too busy with his duties as 'captain' of the ship."

Tom noticed that she used her fingers to put air quotes around the word captain. "Yeah, sure. We can work out later on deck," he told her. Then he folded his arms and went back to the subject of his brother. "So . . . it sounds to me like you don't agree with Captain Mitch's action plan."

"No, I don't," said Laura. "I tried to talk to him at breakfast, but he wouldn't listen."

"Like he did to me last night," Tom murmured. He ran a hand through his hair. It felt damp. "So I missed breakfast?"

Laura answered by pulling a popular Japanese-made energy bar out of her back pocket and tossing it to him. Tom caught it, unwrapped the bright green foil, and swallowed the entire thing within seconds.

"Rough night, huh?" Laura asked. "Your hair looks wet. Were you sweating?"

"Yeah, guess I was," he said.

"We tried to get you up an hour ago," Laura said, "but you were really out of it. Major REMs going down."

"I had another dream," he admitted.

Laura frowned. "You okay?"

"Pointless question." Tom wiped his mouth with the back of his hand and grabbed a bottle of water off his dresser. "I'm not the one in danger."

"I know," said Laura. She shook her head, walked across Tom's cabin, and peered out the huge porthole at the small deserted island.

"I can't stop worrying about Emiko," she confessed.

"She was so sweet to me, from the very first day at Matsu School. Now my mind just keeps replaying the image of that punk grabbing her off the street, dragging her away on his motorcycle. . . . "

"Kunio will pay for that." Tom's fingers tightened around the bottled water. "I can't wait to get my hands on that jerk."

Kunio Matsu was the cousin of Nikki Matsu. Both teens were tied into the activities of their family's Tokyo-based company, but they'd recently taken different paths. While Nikki had grown to distrust Julian Vane, suspecting him of dark maneuverings as her father's new partner, Kunio had become enamored with the billionaire.

That's why Nikki had decided to help Tom and Mitch, and loaned them this ship—while Kunio was doing Vane's bidding, playing a gangster-wannabe with the Black Lotus crew.

"I just want to reach back in time," said Laura. "I want to change the way it happened that night; grab Emiko back. Save my friend, you know?"

She turned to face Tom. He rubbed the back of his neck, wishing he could say something that would make her feel better, but he was stumped.

Laura shook her head. "I hate this! The whole thing just makes me feel so . . . so . . . helpless."

Helpless, Tom repeated to himself. He thought of his own visionary dreams of the Dragon, the boys, and Julian Vane. The recurring trips to Dragon Island in his dreams—but never in reality—were so frustrating he wanted to scream.

"Believe me, Laura," he finally told her, "I know exactly how you feel."

CHAPTER 3

Beep . . . Beep . . . Beep . . .

"What is that?" Mitch asked. "I've been on this bridge for hours, and that's the first time I've heard that noise."

Brian shrugged. "That's because we've been in hydrofoil mode. Now, we're just anchored off an island, so the hull's back in the water. The fish finder will be going off more often."

"Fish finder?"

"Yeah, look . . ." Brian pointed to one of the many computer screens on the high-tech control panel. A graphic showed a white object, moving in a field of blue. A digital rule on one side of the screen showed the object's depth.

"Something's moving just under the water a few kilometers away," said Brian, pointing to the white object.

26

"How big?"

"Not very. Could be a school of fish. Or more likely a whale. Didn't Laura mention she liked whales? We should tell her to look over the port side, maybe she'll see it surfacing."

"We don't have time to whale watch," Mitch snapped. "My brother was right about one thing last night. We shouldn't waste time. So turn down the volume on that fish finder, and let's round up Laura and Tom. We need to start searching that island."

"How do you want to execute the search?" Brian asked, punching buttons on the control panel's keyboard.

"We'll launch a motorized skiff," said Mitch. He began to pace. "Mr. Chance can stay on board the *Rakurai*. And you, me, Tom, and Laura will stay in touch by radio. Then we'll divide up the shoreline as soon as we land."

"Divide up how?"

"We'll work in teams," explained Mitch. "You and Tom will start walking east. Me and Laura will walk west. The whole island's just one big three-mile oval. We should be able to walk it completely and meet up on the other side in under an hour."

"That all sounds very methodical," Brian said, "except for one tiny little glitch."

"Glitch?" Mitch stopped pacing and frowned. "What glitch?"

"It seems very wrong to pair me with Tom," said Brian. "He doesn't like me very much. And he has quite a temper. Who knows what could happen if I say the wrong thing? He might kill me!"

Mitch rolled his eyes. "Fine. You take Laura."

"Yes! Me and Laura paired up together. That's what I had in mind all along." Brian grinned as if Mitch had just given him a birthday present, all wrapped up with a bow on top. "Thanks!"

"Don't thank me yet," warned Mitch.

"Why not?"

"Laura has a temper too. If I were you, I'd be very careful not to tick her off."

侍

"So . . . what are we looking for exactly?" Tom asked his brother as they hiked along the beach. He paused to take a swig from his water bottle.

Mitch exhaled and kept walking. He didn't bother turning around to answer. Tom had asked the same question five different ways in the last twenty minutes, and he was getting sick of explaining himself.

"I mean it, Mitch, what am I supposed to be finding here on the Isle of Nowheresville? Or did you want to name it something in Latin?"

Mitch groaned. Under any other circumstances, he would have enjoyed this trip. The island itself was quite beautiful. To his left were the blue waters of the Pacific Ocean. They lapped a pristine white strip of sand peppered with black stones as shiny as patent leather and millions of pink and blue seashells. Giant palm trees grew to his right, a columnlike edge to an intriguing tangle of thick vegetation.

"Hey, Mitch," Tom called again to his brother's back. "Maybe the type of stones on the beach are some sort of clue? They look like volcanic rock, by the way. How about the species of palm trees? Wait a second! Mitch, look!"

For a moment Tom's voice actually sounded sincere, so Mitch finally turned around to see what his brother wanted. "What is it?" he asked.

"Up there!" Tom said urgently.

The vegetation was plenty thick beyond the shoreline. Tom pointed to one of the many trees on the edge of the beach.

"What is it?" asked Mitch, shading his eyes. "What do you see?"

"I think there's a suspicious coconut on that tree," Tom whispered. "Maybe we should check it for surveillance devices."

Clenching his fists, Mitch stalked up to his twin. Mitch prided himself on his coolness and patience, but Tom had been goading him since they'd left the *Rakurai* and motored to shore.

"I've just about had enough of your attitude, you know that?" Mitch snapped.

Tom went nose-to-nose with his brother. "That makes two of us."

"You're being insubordinate!"

"Oh, really? Well, what are you going to do about it, *Captain*? Make me walk the plank?" Tom's eyes narrowed. "How about an old-fashioned flogging?"

Mitch threw down his backpack. "How about it? It might improve your attitude."

"It might." Tom dropped his own pack and shoved Mitch's shoulder. "But who's going to give it to me?"

That did it. "Aaaaahhh!" Mitch launched himself at his brother with a flurry of hand strikes.

Mitch was a good martial artist, and basic training had made him better, but he was fighting with anger now, not tactics, so his series of straight jabs were well telegraphed. Tom defended himself with ease.

For a while, Tom refrained from retaliating, and simply continued moving backward with Mitch's every advance. But a sweet opening finally presented itself, and Tom couldn't resist. He delivered a perfect right cross to his brother's jaw.

Smack!

Mitch cried out, more in surprise than pain. The strike stung, all right, but he knew it was nowhere near what his brother was capable of delivering. In R.O.N.I.N. basic training, instruments had recorded Tom's thrusts as hard enough to break bones.

Mitch reeled from the strike, but he refused to put an end to their sparring. Tom could pull all the punches he wanted, but Mitch was determined to teach him a lesson.

Using the momentum of the hit, Mitch exaggerated his response, wheeling completely around. With a surprise drop, he swept his left leg in a hard arc, slamming Tom in the back of his calves for a perfectly executed sweep.

"Crap!" Tom yelled as his legs were knocked out from under him. He hit the rocky beach with an *"Ooof!"*

Mitch scrambled to pin him down, but Tom was too fast. Like a world-class gymnast, he tucked and flexed, launching from his prone position back up to his feet.

Mitch jumped backward, crouching into a fighting stance: Arms up, his side facing his opponent, Mitch waited for the next attack.

Tom didn't bother. He stepped over to his dropped backpack, grabbed his water bottle, and took a long swig.

"You done?" Mitch asked, still crouched and ready.

"You?" Tom replied. He swallowed more water, wiped his mouth with the back of his hand, and then shook his head.

Mitch took a breath, then began to drop his arms and straighten his posture. That's when Tom launched. Dropping the bottle, he rushed in for a judo throw. He grabbed his brother by his left wrist, spun into his body, and tossed him over his right shoulder.

"Ooof!" Now it was Mitch's turn to land hard.

Tom moved to pin him, but Mitch rolled and kicked out with his left leg. Tom parried with his arm, but Mitch expected he would. That kick was a fake-out. The real attack came from his other leg, which he hooked under Tom's ankle.

"No . . ." Tom felt the assault on his balance. He didn't go down, but it took him three steps to recover.

Mitch used the time to leap back to his feet—not as elegantly as his brother, but just as fast. He lunged immediately, launching another series of hand strikes.

Tom moved backward with the expert assault, countering every strike. His retaliations were few, as he still seemed to be having trouble regaining his balance.

Mitch noticed a collection of fallen palm trees a few meters away. Continuing his forward assault, he moved Tom toward the rotting trunks, hoping to trip him up.

But before he got there, Tom telegraphed a powerful kick. Sloppy, Mitch thought with disdain. He moved to block, but instead found himself reeling from another jaw strike—harder than the first. Tom's sloppy kick had been a total fake-out!

"Aaaah!" Mitch cried out.

Tom laughed. "Nobody can think but *you*, right, Captain?"

"And *you* can't stand to follow a leader!"

Mitch lunged with handwork again, but his attempted strikes were all ploys. He gradually lured Tom closer. He waited until Tom's perfect right cross came straight at him. But this time Mitch was ready. Dodging the strike, he dropped and swept Tom's legs for a second time.

"Argh!" Tom was ticked that he hadn't seen that one coming *again*.

Mitch laughed as he swiftly moved in. His brother was flat on his back and ready for the kill. But Tom was faking once more. When Mitch moved over him, he grabbed his brother's shirt, tucked his knees, and threw Mitch with a thrust of his legs. Mitch went up, then down, slamming to the beach on his back.

Tom pinned him immediately. "Check!" he cried.

Mitch narrowed his eyes on Tom's cocked hand, fingers curled, palm angled forward. One strategically placed strike was all it would take, and he knew it.

"Say it," said Tom.

"Get off," growled Mitch.

"Say it, brother."

"Checkmate, okay? Now get off me!"

Both boys were breathing hard. The two had sparred plenty over the years, but this wasn't a workout, it was a grudge match, and the grudge was far from over.

CHAPTER 4

Tom released his brother and walked back to his pack for his water bottle. "Just admit it, Mitch. We shouldn't have wasted time coming here—"

"Stop it. Stop complaining." Mitch rose from the ground, brushing sand and tiny stones off his jeans. "If you want to go back to the ship, go. But I'm going to keep looking for—"

"Hey, what is this?" Tom exclaimed. He bent low and picked something up off the ground. "Mitch, I think I found something."

"Please. No more coconut surveillance device jokes," said Mitch. "I can't take it anymore."

"Shut up. Look at this." Tom held out a green foil sleeve with Japanese characters on it.

Mitch snatched the find. "It looks like a candy bar wrapper."

"It's a sesame-flavored energy bar, a popular brand

in Tokyo. Laura just gave me one for breakfast."

"So?" Mitch held the wrapper out to his brother in disgust. "You shouldn't be littering. Even on a deserted island—"

"No, Mitch! It's not mine! I threw mine away in the cabin. This must have been left here by someone else."

Mitch automatically glanced up to locate Laura and Brian. But they were at least a mile down the beach by now. Their skiff was tied up halfway between them. They hadn't come near this area of the shoreline. They'd begun walking east while Tom and Mitch had been walking west.

"Dr. Gensai?" Mitch questioned.

"Or someone else from Japan," said Tom.

Mitch nodded. "Let's look around some more."

Tom quickly nodded, and for the next few minutes, the two worked together. They marked off quadrants of the beach area and began to scan it for evidence like a crime scene.

Before long, they found something else, something much more significant than a discarded food wrapper. Camouflaged within the fallen palm tree trunks was a thick pole about two feet high. It appeared to be man-made and was embedded deep in the ground.

"Look at this!" Tom cried excitedly. "What is it?"

"I'm not sure." Mitch frowned. He looked more

closely at the top of the pole. "Wait . . . these are solar panels."

"Solar panels?" said Tom, scratching his head. "Why would anyone install solar panels on a deserted island?"

"To power something. Besides, who said it's deserted?"

"You think someone's here?" Tom asked.

"I don't know," Mitch replied, eyeing the tiny screws on the side of the solar panels, "but I'm going to find out. Throw me my backpack."

"Sure," said Tom, walking away. "But why?" he called over his shoulder.

"I've got a tool kit in there." Mitch clapped his hands and rubbed them together. "Time for a little exploratory hardware surgery."

侍

"Can you read me?" asked a voice in Japanese. The words crackled over the mini-submarine's transmitter.

"I can read you," replied the man in the jungle.

"Good." More crackling followed, and then the mini-sub's transmitter carried the Japanese voice again. "Are you ready?"

"Almost." The man in the jungle lifted his binoculars and peered out through the thick vegetation. "We identified the group as soon as they hit the beach. The brothers went east, the boy and girl west."

"Be careful of the brothers," said the voice from the mini-sub. "They're more trouble than they look."

"So I've heard."

"And one last thing," added the voice. "Make sure there's sufficient space to maneuver before you strike."

"Affirmative."

侍

"I don't know what's gotten into Mitch," said Laura as she walked down the island's beach.

Brian scratched his head. "What do you mean?"

"What do you mean, what do I mean?" Laura replied. "He's become a tyrant. Haven't you noticed? Since Mr. Chance made him captain, he's always barking orders. He's completely alienated his own brother!"

Brian shrugged. "He's just trying to be a good leader."

"Uh-huh."

Laura squinted up at the bright sun. It might have felt too hot, but the stiff Pacific island breeze was keeping the shoreline cool. The wind ruffled her shorts and ponytail. She searched the shoreline and spotted Tom and Mitch. They'd started out together twenty minutes ago. Now they looked so far away—at least a mile.

"Listen, Brian, late last night, after we all went to bed, I went back to examining the memory crystal

Emiko dropped back at the Mount Fuji facility—"

"Dropped, you say?" Brian interrupted. "Or do you think maybe she left it behind on purpose, as a clue to let someone know she was being held there?"

"Emiko's smart enough to have done it on purpose, but either way, that's not my point." Laura pulled the crystal out from under her tank top. She wore it on a silver chain all the time now. "We examined this after our raid, and we know the device definitely belonged to Emiko Gensai. That's what we determined from the initial analysis of the data."

"I know that."

"Well here's something you don't know. Last night I found some really odd data on the necklace too—a long string of programming code I couldn't decipher or figure out a use for."

Brian nodded, interested. "I could take a look at it for you."

"Great. I was at the top of my class in computer science back at my school in New York. But Emiko's ten times more advanced than me, which means you're probably fifty times more." Laura sighed. "That's tough to admit, but there it is."

Brian grinned with pride. "Doesn't it feel good to get the truth off your chest?"

Laura rolled her eyes. Brian was such an arrogant

nerd! "So anyway, I think you ought to spend some time with this crystal and *also* with Dr. Gensai's laptop."

"But Mitch is working on that. And I'd rather spend time with you, Laura."

Laura stiffened. Brian was supposed to be hung up on Emiko. Now he was giving her big puppy-dog eyes. The needle on her geek-crush-o-meter had just jumped into the red zone.

Yuck, she thought. I'd better derail this train before it gets anywhere near the station!

"Look, Brian," she said, "I know Mitch ordered you to monitor all the ship's programming, and I know he thinks that old, wrinkled map of Gensai's has all the info he needs. But I think the data on the laptop is more important."

"You said that at breakfast. . . ." Brian shook his head. "Mitch doesn't agree."

"I know! And he won't listen. He's being a total jerk!"

"Try to see it from his point of view, Laura. Mitch is responsible for running that huge ship."

Brian turned and gestured to the *Rakurai*, anchored in the distance. Then he shook his head and stared off into the horizon.

"He's *also* trying to take down Julian Vane, save Emiko, her dad, and all the other missing people, including his own dad, and on top of all that, he's trying to locate some island he's confided in me that he's not even sure exists!" Brian added. "That's real pressure. The dude's doing his best. I think we should cut him some slack."

"You forget, Brian. My father's been missing too. And what do you mean he's not even sure that Dragon Island exists? Since when did he start doubting his brother's visions—"

Laura's words were suddenly cut off. A muffled scream followed.

Brian wheeled back around to find Laura being lifted off the ground. A canvas bag had been dropped over her. Legs kicking frantically, she was hoisted into the air by a motley collection of tattooed, savage-looking thugs. Brian stepped backward as two of the thugs swiftly approached him. He knew what Tom or Mitch would do at a moment like this, but he was no martial artist. Instead of fighting, he simply froze.

"Do you know who we are?" one of the men asked him in Japanese.

Gaping in total shock, Brian swallowed. "Pirates," he whispered.

CHAPTER 5

A mile away from Brian and Laura, Mitch remained focused on his and Tom's discovery. Crouching on the beach, he removed the covering solar panels on the two-foot pole and began to examine the object's interior.

"What is it?" Tom asked, standing over him.

"I'm not sure, but there's a computer in here. And the fine print indicates that this equipment was manufactured by Matsu Cybernetics Corporation."

Tom nodded. "Dr. Gensai was doing research for Matsu, wasn't he?"

"That's right." Mitch reached for his handheld computer. He searched the electronics inside the pole for anything resembling a USB port. "Got it!"

"Got what?" Tom crouched down next to his brother.

"A connecting port. See . . . ," said Mitch, showing Tom. He plugged the wire into his handheld computer.

"I'll download any available data in this thing's memory drive and analyze it back on the ship."

"And you're looking for . . . ?"

"A lot of things," said Mitch. "The data should be able to tell me exactly what this equipment is supposed to do, and how recently it was installed—"

"Nooooooooo! Aaaahhhhh!"

"What the . . . ?" Mitch's head snapped up. "That was Laura."

"Yeah," said Tom. "I heard her too."

"Aaaahhhhh! Noooooooo! Heeeeeeelp!"

Laura's screams were far away, but they were clearly traveling on the wind.

"Get a visual," Mitch commanded.

Tom lunged for his backpack, pulled out his binoculars. "Men on the beach," he reported, peering through the glass. "They've got Laura and Brian!"

Mitch disconnected his handheld computer and reached for the walkie-talkie in his pocket. "Mr. Chance, come in. Mr. Chance!"

While he waited for an answer from the ship, he shaded his eyes, trying to see what was happening. But the action was too far away.

"How many targets?" he asked Tom.

"Seven."

"Are they Black Lotus ninjas?"

"Don't think so. They're dressed in raggedy clothes. Some have tattoos. They look more like—"

"Pirates." Mitch tensed. He suddenly remembered the notation he'd seen on Dr. Gensai's wrinkled map—a notation he'd dismissed as ridiculous and never bothered to share with anyone else.

"I don't see a ship," said Tom, "not even a skiff."

"Their boat could be on the other side of the island."

"Is Mr. Chance answering?" Tom asked, still looking through his binoculars.

"Not yet."

"We can't wait for him," cried Tom. "Let's go!"

Tossing his binoculars, he took off down the beach. Mitch followed, running after him.

"Tom, hold up!"

"What for?" Tom called over his shoulder. He slowed but refused to stop.

"Those pirates haven't seen us coming yet. If we get off the beach, move through the jungle, we can surprise them. We need to stop and make a plan!"

"What we need to do is act. Laura and Brian could be kidnapped or killed. Moving through that tangle of vegetation will just slow us down. There's no time for anything but a direct assault."

"But—"

"No time for 'buts,' either! Come on!"

Mitch hailed Mr. Chance one more time as they ran, but Tom was breaking away. He'd have to push to keep up. Pocketing his walkie-talkie, Mitch pumped his legs into high gear.

Brian was terrified. He didn't want to get hurt, and he certainly didn't want them to hurt Laura.

So far, she seemed okay. After covering her with a canvas bag, three of the seven pirates carried her about twenty feet away and tied a rope around her arms and legs.

She was thrashing around on the ground, screaming as loudly as she could. But the three pirates didn't appear to care about her screaming. At first one of them kicked her, but then another one shouted something, and the assault stopped. Now they were just standing nearby, as if guarding her.

The remaining four pirates stood in front of Brian. There was no bag for him, however, and that was why he began to shake.

Swick! Two of the pirates opened switchblades. One man was short with an unkempt beard. The other was much taller. He wore a red kerchief on his head and had a jagged scar down his cheek. The other two were about average height and build. They all appeared to be Japanese. All were barefoot, too, and wore ratty clothes—soiled shirts and raggedy pants.

Brian felt his breakfast coming up on him. Are they going to kill me? he wondered, gawking at the open switchblades. Are they going to gut me? Or just slit my throat?

Arms limp at his side, Brian bowed several times to the men. "If you please," he told them in Japanese, "do not hurt the girl. If you please!"

The men laughed. "Which girl?" the short one with the beard taunted. "The one in the bag, or the one standing before us?"

Brian bowed again. "I would not presume to argue with you, Mr. Pirate. But, you know, a girl like this one, she's worth very little. If you release her, I could trade you. I could provide you with something that would make you much richer! Much!"

"Hmmm . . . ," said the short one, glancing at his companions. "This girlie wants to make a deal."

The four pirates laughed again.

"I think we should hear him out," declared the tall one with the red kerchief on his head and the scar down his cheek. "Keep talking," he told Brian. "Tell us what you have in mind."

CHAPTER 6

As Tom ran the long mile down the beach, he focused on the seven pirates menacing his friends.

A year ago he never would have assumed that he and his brother could take on seven opponents in a hand-to-hand battle. But then he'd been through a lot in the last few months. . . .

"Attack with accuracy. Attack with speed. Attack with confidence."

These were the lessons Tom's combat sensei had drilled into him during R.O.N.I.N. basic.

"Fear, hesitation . . . strike these words from your vocabulary. . . ."

Tom remembered the hard months of work; ten- and twelve-hour days of sparring; simulations with one opponent, then two; then four and eight. He remembered learning techniques against opponents with weapons; against black belts in judo, kung fu, savate, aikido, and

Korean karate. And most of all, what Tom remembered about combat training was his very first day. . . .

BASIC TRAINING
A REMOTE AREA OF JAPAN
"Show me how you fight."

Tom's combat sensei was a well-built yet elderly Chinese man. Mr. Chance called this man "Panther." Tom was warned never to call him anything but "Sensei."

Panther stood before Tom in black pants, legs braced. His lean and muscled chest was bare.

"Show me how you fight," Panther repeated to Tom. He began to move around the mat, circling his only student.

"Hand or foot drill, Sensei?" asked Tom. He felt funny standing there all alone with one instructor, in the middle of the empty dojo.

For the previous three weeks, Tom had been taking classes with Mitch and Laura. Their mornings had been filled with brutal obstacle courses and body building. Their afternoons had been occupied with lessons in map reading, advanced technology, and communications. Then the fourth week came, and the three teenagers were told they'd been evaluated and would now train separately.

"Uh, Sensei, you don't actually want me to attack

you, do you?" Tom asked Panther. "I mean—"

Panther dropped and swept Tom's legs. With an "*Ooof*," Tom fell to the mat, and Panther moved over him for the kill. Tom finally got the idea. He rolled and leaped back to his feet, facing Panther in the ready position.

Panther moved in again. Tom lashed out, using the hand strikes and kicks he'd learned from his ten years of lessons back in New York. He knew his form was perfect, absolutely correct, yet none of his strikes were connecting.

"You're afraid," Panther coolly declared, as his muscular forearms blocked every one of Tom's attacks.

"I'm not!"

"You're striking from too far away, without confidence."

Tom tried harder to hit Panther. It didn't help. Panther continued to counter Tom's advances with ease, then finally moved in and used another judo sweep to put Tom flat on his back. Panther's hand was now poised in a perfect killing stroke, right under Tom's nose.

"You aren't trying hard enough to win," said the sensei. "You are merely trying not to lose." Rising from the mat, he folded his arms. "From what I see, you have had *no* training."

"That's not true!" Tom protested, sitting up. "I studied for more than ten years in New York. I earned a black belt in—"

"On your feet!"

Still on the mat, Tom took a deep breath. Okay, don't freak, he counseled himself. You can hang in there with this dude. Just get back to the ready position.

Tom took his time rising. He turned his back on Panther and began stepping across the mat, moving to the position he'd been taught to take for a match. Once he was ready, he would wait for Panther's signal to begin sparring.

But Panther didn't wait. Seconds after Tom turned his back on his sensei, a stinging strike came to the back of his neck.

Tom cursed. Panther had hit him from behind! "That's a foul!" he yelled.

"Do you think you are in a tournament?" asked Panther. "Do you think this is a game?"

Before Tom could answer, his sensei struck out

again, delivering a stinging blow to Tom's ribs.

"Aaaah!" Tom doubled over in pain.

Inside of two minutes, Panther had evaluated Tom's previous decade of training with one sentence. "You never learned martial arts."

"I did, Sensei, I worked hard in New York. I—"

"You worked on a mechanical repetition of a fixed pattern of movements. But martial arts, like any art, should be a fluid expression."

"I don't understand."

"*Sensei*," Panther corrected.

"I'm sorry." Tom bowed. "I don't understand, Sensei."

"Like life, Tom, martial arts is an ongoing process of flow, discovery, actualization, and expansion. It requires true wakefulness as one moves through the world and unflinching honesty in the scrutiny of oneself."

Tom shook his head. "I still don't understand."

"You will," said Panther, pacing the mat as gracefully as his namesake. "You will learn to use your eyes and ears—*all* of your senses. You will learn ancient methods of focus, methods that will allow you to be in total control of your body, even its autonomic functions. You will learn techniques from many schools so that you may evaluate your opponent in the blink of an eye and adapt to any situation with *whatever* fighting technique is useful. And you will learn to do all of this instinctively."

Tom stared, wide-eyed. As a rule, he'd always been a pretty cocky dude—even when he felt unsure of himself, he could usually bluff his way through things. But all alone in the dojo with Panther, he truly didn't think he was capable of learning any of that stuff. Still . . . Tom wouldn't quit. Not when his father's life could depend on it.

"Yes, Sensei," he whispered.

Panther suddenly stopped pacing. He faced Tom and put a hand on his shoulder. When he spoke again, his voice was softer, kinder. "What I am charged with teaching you, Tom, is not a sport. It will save your life and the lives of others—*if* you are willing to learn it."

Panther took his hand away. His voice grew hard again. "Are you willing to learn it, Tom?"

"Yes, Sensei!"

侍

What Tom learned in the days that followed wasn't magic. He knew very well that he and his brother weren't invincible. They could lose; they could get hurt or killed. But Tom had learned not to dwell on that.

Now he felt fully prepared as he sprinted with his brother down the rock-strewn sand of the island beach. He was completely ready to confront seven grown men.

Tom focused as he ran, the way Panther had taught him, not on the battle, but on the tranquility of the jade dragon. The Dragon's talons were fierce, but his expression was calm. And like the Dragon, Tom became calm.

This wasn't like sparring with his brother, this was real combat; and the closer he came to the battle ground, the sharper Tom's focus became. His pulse slowed, his heartbeat became steady as a drum, and his hearing and vision grew razor sharp.

One task and one task alone now occupied Tom's physical and mental being: Stop the men who were threatening his friends.

CHAPTER 7

As Brian continued trying to reason with the tattooed thugs, he noticed two figures running toward them.

Tom and Mitch, he realized. They were moving like bullets down the shoreline.

Brian knew he was no fighter. Physical fitness was beyond him—he didn't even like to walk fast! But he could do one important thing to help the boys. He could sufficiently distract their opponents.

The longer I keep these thugs looking east, the better chance Tom and Mitch have of attacking them from the west.

"I know where you can find solid gold bars!" Brain bragged to the pirates. "Millions of dollars' worth, ready for the taking!"

"Oh, really?" said the pirate with the unkempt beard. "And where might these gold bars be? Under your granny's mattress or under your Hello Kitty pillow?"

The pirates laughed.

That's right, you idiots, thought Brian, bowing again. Keep laughing at me. Just as long as you keep looking at me!

Finally the tall pirate with the jagged scar on his cheek said, "Enough. Let's get on with our business."

He stepped up to Brian, knife in hand. Brian gulped and shook, closing his eyes, preparing for the worst.

But the pirate didn't touch him. He didn't punch him, kick him, or slice him. All he did was start talking to him.

The man kept his voice low, as if he didn't want Laura to hear what he was saying. Not that she could. She was still trapped in that canvas bag, and she'd never stopped screaming.

Brian was stunned by the news the pirate was now delivering to him. He didn't want to believe the man, and he told him so.

The tall pirate just smiled, the flash of a gold tooth shining in the sun. He reached into the pocket of his raggedy pants and dangled evidence to support his claim.

Brian took the dog tags from the pirate. He examined them closely and realized, with a sickening feeling, that he had to believe what this man was telling him. The evidence he held was impossible to dispute.

Racing beside his brother, Mitch flexed his hands.

"You ready?" he called to Tom.

"Yeah, bro," Tom replied. "Let's get 'em."

Mitch nodded with relief. His brother could be difficult at times, but he was an extremely dangerous opponent, and Mitch definitely preferred Tom watching his back instead of painting a target on it.

Mitch quickly took in the battle space—three men were standing over Laura, who was still on the ground with a bag over her head, ropes tied around her. Twenty feet away, four more were facing Brian, who appeared to be talking with them.

"Four or three?" Mitch called to his brother.

"Four," said Tom.

Tom knew his brother was talking about the opponent

clusters. They'd learned about that back in basic. Tom was a better fighter than Mitch, and both of them knew it, so Tom stepped up to take the extra man.

Tom noticed that two of his four opponents were waving switchblades. He smiled, recalling what his sensei had told him about weapons.

"When you see a man with a weapon, smile."

"Smile?" Tom had asked.

"Yes, because it is a gift."

"How can that be, sensei?"

"When a man holds a weapon, you already know how he plans to attack you, and with what hand he is most likely to strike. . . . "

侍

Brian's eyes widened at the sight of Tom and Mitch descending on the pirates. The speed at which the brothers launched looked almost supernatural.

As Mitch engaged the three men standing over Laura, Tom sailed through the air like a bird. Two of the four pirates were standing close together. With a single scissors kick, he knocked each of them out cold—one with the left leg, the other with the right.

As the men fell to the beach, Tom landed and immediately sprang into the air again, this time with a wheeling spin-kick. His target was the third pirate—the short one with the unkempt beard and switchblade.

The man was lunging to stab Tom, but Tom struck the man's hand first, sending the switchblade sailing into the ocean waters.

"Whoa," Brian whispered.

By now the tall pirate with the scar realized that they were under attack. He turned with his own blade open, ready to slice Tom across the torso.

"Tom, behind you!" cried Brian.

But Tom was already aware of the tall pirate's movements. He wheeled again powerfully, whipping his forearm into a hard block. Then he grabbed hold of the man's wrist, counterstriking with the other hand.

Brian shuddered at the sound of the arm bone breaking. The man screamed in pain, fell to his knees, and dropped his switchblade.

Tom kicked the knife toward Brian. As he lunged to pick it up, Tom wheeled for another spin-kick, knocking the screaming, scar-faced pirate unconscious.

The final, bearded renegade stood a few feet away, crouched in a fighting position. Tom had sent the man's switchblade flying into the ocean, but he was still rooted to the spot, frantically searching for backup among his companions.

The three thugs around the bearded pirate were now out cold. And the cluster of brutes by Laura weren't there anymore. Two of those men were down and the third was running away, thanks to Mitch, who was now rushing over to back up his brother.

Tom advanced on the bearded man, who nervously attempted a few hand strikes before Tom moved in, taking hold of the man's raggedy shirt and tossing him over his shoulder in an expert judo throw.

The bearded pirate cursed as he hit the beach. He rolled and attempted to kick out as Mitch approached. Mitch was kept at bay, but only for a few seconds.

The pirate had had enough. Screaming curses in Japanese, he scrambled to his feet and ran down the sunny shoreline. He veered into the trees for cover, where he was swallowed up by the darkening shade of the jungle's shadows.

侍

"Let me out of this stupid sack!" Laura yelled.

"Allow me." Brian used the recovered switchblade to cut Laura loose. He began to help pull the sack off her too, but she was too furious to wait. Shoving the canvas off, she threw it to the ground.

"Creeps!" she cried, springing to her feet, hands raised. "Jerks! Pigs! Where are they? I want to kick their butts!"

"Sorry to disappoint you, Laura," said Brian, "but their butts have been thoroughly kicked. Mitch and Tom made sure of that."

Steaming mad, Laura glanced around at the bruised,

unconscious pirates. "Well, okay, fine! I'll just make sure these thugs *stay* down!"

Laura was about to start whaling on the first body when Mitch and Tom both took an arm.

"Hold up," said Tom. "Calm down."

"Yeah, Laura," Mitch chimed in. "Find your center or something."

"Center schmenter! *You* weren't the ones stuffed in a stinky sack and kicked. If it was up to me, those guys would no longer be breathing!"

"Well, they are," said Mitch. "And two of them ran away."

"Where?" asked Laura.

"Off into the jungle," Brian said, pointing.

"So we better get out of here," said Mitch.

"Mitch is right," Tom agreed. "For once."

Mitch smirked. "So we're back to backhanded remarks again, are we?"

"You can give me a court-martial later, okay?" said Tom. "Right now, we need to get back to the ship. We don't know if those two ran off for reinforcements or what."

Laura broke away from their hold. "Tom's right. I'm calm now. Let's go."

As the four of them began jogging down the beach, Mitch finally made contact with Mr. Chance.

Chance immediately motored out to meet the

teenagers. He steered the second skiff close to the shoreline, then Laura and Brian waded into the surf and climbed aboard.

While Mr. Chance idled the motor on his boat, Tom and Mitch retrieved their packs and waded out to the first skiff. Then all of them motored back to the anchored *Rakurai*.

As they skimmed along the choppy blue waves, Tom turned to Mitch. "I didn't want to say anything until we were alone."

"Say what?" asked Mitch, steering the boat.

"Don't you think it was odd how seven pirates took Laura down right away, but they let Brian just stand there? They never bothered bagging him, tying him up, or touching one hair on his head. All they did was talk to him. Why do you suppose that is?"

"They probably saw right away that he wasn't a threat. Brian's got a brilliant mind when it comes to technology, but he's not exactly a force to be reckoned with—physically. I mean, the guy's instant message ID is CuddleBuddy."

"My point exactly. Why did those seven pirates decide that talking to Brian was worth their time?"

"I don't know," said Mitch with a shrug. "You'd have to ask him—but please don't. He already thinks you don't like him."

"I don't trust him. There's a difference."

"Whatever. Just chill, okay? The pirate thing's over and done with. So let's put it behind us and move along. We certainly have enough on our plate to focus on."

In the other skiff, Mr. Chance was busy steering the craft toward the *Rakurai*'s hull. Laura was occupied checking the bruises on her arms and legs. Neither noticed Brian angling away from both of them.

Digging deep into the pocket of his khaki pants, Brian closed his hand around the set of military dog tags the scarred pirate had given him. He pulled the tags out and examined them again.

Tears came to Brian's eyes as he fingered the U.S. Navy tags, reading their engraved lettering. His father's name, rank, and serial number were all correct.

Wiping his cheeks, Brian resolutely shoved the tags back into his pocket. He knew he had no choice now. Like it or not, Brian would have to do what the pirates demanded. His father's life depended on it.

ON BOARD
THE RAKURAI . . .

WE SHOULD BE TRACKING DOWN JULIAN VANE, NOT WASTING TIME LOOKING FOR AN ISLAND!

BEWARE OF PIRATES!

HEY, MITCH, THAT COCONUT LOOKS SUSPICIOUS.

PIRATES!

I KNOW WHERE YOU CAN FIND SOLID GOLD BARS!

CREEPS! WHERE ARE THEY?

THAT'S GOOD NEWS, KUNIO.

WE FOUND A GEOTHERMAL SENSOR.

MITCH DOUBTS THAT DRAGON ISLAND EXISTS!

WHAT IF DRAGON ISLAND EXISTS BUT DOESN'T EXIST?

BRIAN'S GONE!

WE'RE UNDER ATTACK!

THE SHOTS WERE COMING FROM THAT SHIP.

WE HAVE TO SURRENDER!

CHAPTER 8

COMMUNICATIONS NEEDLE
VANE ISLAND, PACIFIC OCEAN

Kunio Matsu stepped out of the richly paneled elevator. A giant security guard in a crimson uniform glanced down at him.

"Mr. Vane is expecting me," Kunio said, careful to keep his hands respectfully at his sides, his eyes downcast.

Kunio was a wiry teen with lean, hard muscles and a jagged attitude, but Julian Vane's security guard stood at almost twice his height and three times his width.

"You can wait at the bar," said the guard, folding his brawny arms.

Kunio stepped around the giant and strode into the main living area of the plush apartment. This was only the second time he'd been summoned to Vane's private suite of rooms in the Communications Needle, but he remembered every detail: European-made furnishings, Persian prayer rugs, and beautiful female servants.

With greedy eyes, Kunio drank in the German-engineered entertainment console and jewel-encrusted sculptures. Beyond the large living space was Vane's personal sundeck. Soaring hundreds of feet in the air, it ringed the saucer-shaped perimeter of the Needle's main structure, giving the tycoon a stupefying view of the blue-green Pacific.

Built to resemble Seattle's Space Needle, Vane's massive tower had been completed only recently on this small, volcanic plot. The Needle reached into the clouds with the most powerful broadcasting antenna known to man. At its center, a superfast elevator speared five saucer-shaped floors that housed computer labs filled with cutting-edge communications technology.

One quadrant of the Needle's highest level held Vane's private apartment. Walking across its spacious living room, Kunio noticed something interesting being broadcast on Vane's dozen flat-screen plasma televisions. The screens showed famous pop music artists in rehearsal on vast arena stages all over the world.

"Cool," murmured Kunio, taking a seat at the mahogany bar.

The muted images were part of direct live feeds

coming from at least five of Vane's satellites. The pop artists were rehearsing for Vane's upcoming World Concert for Freedom.

The concert had been in the planning stages for many months. Funded by Vane, the event was being billed as an Olympics of music, with hundreds of performers in dozens of nations.

Kunio recognized all of the artists on Vane's monitors, but screen number six held the most interest for him. Ex-Rated was finishing a microphone check at Madison Square Garden.

Ex was the most popular rap star on Julian Vane's Doin' Time music label, and when he began to perform, Kunio reached for a remote on the bar. Turning up screen six's volume, he began mouthing lyrics along with the rapper.

侍

Suddenly he felt a tap on his arm. Kunio turned to find a stunningly beautiful Russian woman behind the bar. She had dark red hair and wore a white bikini. He turned down the volume on the monitor. "Excuse me, Kunio, would you like a drink?" she asked. "How about a coconut cocktail?"

It took Kunio a moment to find his voice. "Yes," he finally said. "That would be fine."

"Whip one up for me as well, Nadia," Vane called to

the barmaid as he moved into the room.

The tanned, muscular billionaire was dressed casually in khaki-colored shorts and a pale pink linen shirt. His head and face were freshly shaved, giving off a faint citrus aroma, and the neck of the shirt was open, displaying a thick gold chain with a Black Lotus medallion.

"Your men have been successful," Kunio told Vane at once, leaping to his feet and bowing.

"Good, that's what I like to hear."

Vane took a seat at the bar. "Sit down, Kunio, tell me more. Details interest me when the news is good."

Kunio nodded and cleared his throat. "Disguised as common pirates, the ninjas located the Matsu vessel and made direct contact with its crew. They successfully delivered your message to Brian Saito."

The barmaid presented the coconut cocktails, and

Vane lifted his in a toast. "Excellent," Vane declared. "Prepare two rooms. We shall soon have guests."

Kunio gulped some of his sweet drink for nerve, and then asked a difficult question. "Is it wise to keep them here, sir? I mean . . . these brothers, they've thwarted your plans in the past."

"All the more reason to secure them on a tight leash," said Vane. "In any case, they will be in good hands. I am making *you* responsible for their security."

"Yes, sir," Kunio replied, but it wasn't a job he wanted. He'd tangled with Tom and Mitch once, and he wasn't looking forward to doing it again. On the other hand, if "security" required squashing those brothers like bugs, he'd do it with glee.

"Like my feeds?" asked Vane, gesturing to the plasma screens and smiling at Ex-Rated's rap. "Catchy beat." He went on, "As you know, in two days' time, we'll be interrupting the World Concert for Freedom with a broadcast of our own."

"I know, sir."

"Our convincing bit of shadow play will throw the nations of Earth into chaos. The avatars are almost ready. They're superb—flawless. Have you seen the girl's work?"

"Yes, Mr. Vane, I saw it when you asked me to, um . . . speak with her." Kunio couldn't help smiling at the memory of menacing that little brat. Bullying her had been a pleasure.

"Well, the girl shaped up right after you had that little talk with her. Of course, threatening to remove limbs from her father while she watched—that may have had something to do with persuading her to complete her task too, don't you think?"

Kunio's smile broadened. "Yes, Mr. Vane."

"Clearly, the girl's a genius at computer graphics. Perhaps I'll keep her here for another year or so—until what she knows is outdated. Then I'll get rid of her." Vane waved his hand dismissively. "Are we done?"

"One last thing, sir," Kunio said, bowing. "I'll need some reliable muscle for the security detail."

"So?" Vane sipped his drink. "Use the ninjas from the pirate job."

"Three of them have broken bones, sir. The brothers—Mitch and Tom—they appeared on the scene while the ninjas were finishing up their little talk with Brian Saito. I'm afraid these men won't be able to serve you for some time."

Vane cursed, then shook his shaved head.

"Fine," he told Kunio. "We'll get you new men." He snapped his fingers at the giant guard, who was still standing in front of the elevator doors. "Ox, take care of Kunio's personnel needs," Vane ordered.

The giant silently nodded.

"Too bad we can't turn these brothers into Black Lotus ninjas," Vane murmured. "They'd certainly be assets. . . ."

侍

The idea of turning the brothers had occurred to Julian Vane before; now he contemplated the idea with renewed interest. After all, he mused, the boys will soon be my guests. . . .

Turning Kunio had been easy enough, but then the boy's father had been Yakuza. Taking what you wanted without apology, bending people to your will—these were not foreign ideas to Kunio. He obviously relished this philosophy.

Julian's own father had not been a member of organized crime. He had not been any kind of criminal, but Julian had somehow grown up with the same greedy desires as Kunio Matsu.

He well remembered his own trying teen years—the relentless hunger to indulge his appetites, the raging need to prove himself, and the impatience with the dullard boys of his own age, so willing to be manipulated.

For a moment, Julian's mind leaped backward in time. He could still vividly recall the day he himself had been turned, the day he'd met his mentor. . . . Much had changed in his life since that fateful day.

侍

ST. GEORGE'S ACADEMY FOR BOYS
CAMBRIDGE, UNITED KINGDOM
THIRTY-FIVE YEARS AGO

"Do you understand the gravity of your offense, Master Vane?"

Julian was fourteen and angry—very angry. He wanted nothing more than to strangle the headmaster with his bare hands, but he remained slumped in the heavy oak chair, masking his rage with an air of aloof superiority.

Mr. Singh regarded Julian across his vast polished desk. The headmaster was a middle-aged man with short silver hair, an olive complexion, and the slightest traces of an East Indian accent. Sighing deeply, he examined Julian's school file.

"For six months you have been providing test answers to a ring of boys at this academy in exchange for favors and money. Is this true?"

"You say it is."

"You have been corrupting your classmates, Master Vane, facilitating an easy path. But this path you offer is a dangerous one. It is a path of dishonesty, of lies."

Young Julian simply shrugged, then glanced out the window of the headmaster's office.

"When I was your age, my grandfather caught me

72

in a lie. Not as bad as this one, but bad enough because it was hurtful. And what he said to me, I'll never forget: 'A lie is like a little worm you release inside yourself. You may not feel its effects, but it eats away at you nonetheless. Release this worm enough times, and the truth of yourself is gradually eaten away.'"

Julian did all he could to keep from bursting out laughing. A lie is a worm? Ridiculous!

"Do you understand what I'm telling you, Master Vane?" asked the headmaster.

"I understand," Julian muttered with a smirk. Then he leaned forward, his expression turning serious. "But what kind of worm do you suppose it is exactly? An earthworm or a bookworm? A tapeworm or a hookworm?"

Without missing a beat, Mr. Singh assured Julian, "It eats everything real, everything true. It will eventually leave you empty inside. And when a man feels empty, he will attempt to fill his life with things that appear to have value. But in the end, he will be left hollow, as hungry as the worm that has eaten him."

"My father lies," Julian answered back. "He lies all the time—in business, to my mother. He seems pretty happy to me. Rich, too. You should know that. He pays my tuition to you on time, doesn't he?"

"That is now a moot point, young man. Over the

last week, I have left six messages for him that your tuition will no longer be needed here, as you are being expelled. It is truly a shame. Your IQ is one of the highest St. George's Academy has ever measured, but we can no longer tolerate your corrupting influence. I have yet to hear back from Mr. Vane. Have you heard anything from your father?"

Julian frowned and looked away.

Mr. Singh turned a page in Julian's student file. "And when is the last time you actually saw your father?"

Julian shifted in his chair. "What does it matter? He sends me plenty of money, makes sure I have everything I want or need."

"I see you spent last summer with cousins in the United States. And last holiday break you remained here on campus. Your father has not bothered to lay eyes on you in more than three years."

"Whatever."

"Mr. Singh, I assume?" The new voice was unfamiliar—quiet yet sharp.

Julian Vane turned to find a stunning woman standing in the doorway of the headmaster's office. The stranger looked like a Hollywood movie star. Her overcoat was made of very fine material, draping beautifully over one arm, and her crimson-colored suit was custom tailored, fitting her trim physique like a leather driving glove. Julian could not see her eyes, as she had on a pair of sunglasses.

"Your father sent me, Julian," the woman said.

"And who are you?" asked Julian suspiciously.

"You may call me Rosso," she replied in a soothing voice. "Your father heard of your expulsion. That is why I am here to collect you."

The stranger had an accent that was difficult for young Julian to guess—it could be European, but perhaps she had been brought up in England?

"I am also prepared to offer you an apprenticeship," Rosso added.

"An apprenticeship?" Julian sat up straighter in his chair.

"You will learn much, and much will be expected of you in return. But I guarantee you will finally get everything you believe you deserve. . . ."

侍

After that day, Vane never again saw his own father, but his apprenticeship with Rosso had taught him many things. He'd become richer than he ever could have dreamed, and he'd learned that money was not the endgame. For people like him and Rosso, it never was.

"Mr. Vane?" called a Scandinavian beauty from a doorway off the main room.

"Yes, Olga, what is it?"

"You have an overseas call. Rosso would like a progress report."

"Rosso?" Kunio quietly repeated, obviously curious.

Julian frowned at the blond bubble brain in the doorway. He was very unhappy that Kunio had overheard that message. Very unhappy.

Vane had always been careful to give those beneath him the impression that he was his own boss, that he ran the show and answered to no one.

"I'll be right there," he told Olga sharply.

He'd deal with her later. As for Kunio . . . He turned and glared at the teenager—a look calculated to belittle him, keep him in his place.

"See about your own business, Kunio," Vane warned. "And *don't* disappoint me."

CHAPTER 9

THE RAKURAI, PACIFIC OCEAN

"It was a geothermal sensor," said Mitch, scanning data on his computer screen.

"What was?" Laura asked, walking onto the bridge with a half-eaten sandwich in her left hand, a bottle of cherry juice in her right.

After the group had returned to the ship, she'd gone straight to the galley for food while the boys had made a beeline to the bridge. They were eager to use the ship's instruments to analyze some sort of retrieved data.

"Before you screamed, Tom and I found a two-foot pole on the beach," Mitch informed her. "There were electronics inside. I downloaded data from its memory."

"Oh," said Laura, taking another massive bite of her sandwich.

Tom smiled, watching her. "What did Mr. Chance

make for you? It must be good."

"Kobe beef with wasabi and bean sprouts," she garbled as she chewed. "Don't worry, he's making plenty more for you three."

"We'll take a break soon," said Mitch from behind one of the bridge's computer keyboards. "This is more important."

"I know," Laura agreed. Then she washed down her food with a gulp of cherry juice. "I just couldn't wait. Who knew getting treated like a sack of potatoes would build up a monster appetite?"

"Screaming does take a lot of energy," Tom noted, folding his arms. "Uses the lungs."

"So does racing a mile down a beach and kicking butt." Laura laughed as she took another bite of sandwich. "Thanks again, you guys."

Tom blushed a little. "No problem."

"You would have done the same for us," said Mitch.

Brian looked away.

Laura froze, mid-chew. That was stupid of me, she thought. I should have thanked Tom and Mitch in private. Now I've made Brian feel bad.

"So Brian . . . ," Tom said, noticing his pensive silence. "I wanted to ask you . . . "

Mitch tensed. He threw Tom an unhappy stare, but his brother ignored it.

"Why didn't the pirates bag you up too?"

Brian eyes shifted nervously. "They wanted to, Tom . . . but, um . . . I was talking to them, you know?"

"No," Tom stated. "I don't know."

Brian started to fidget. He mumbled something incomprehensible, and then he began chattering without stopping to take a breath.

"I knew you two would come, you know? That you'd hear Laura screaming. So I pretended to make a deal with them. I told them I knew where they could find millions in gold if they just let Laura go. They listened long enough to be distracted. I just kept bowing and telling them about finding this treasure. They probably didn't believe me, but they seemed amused by my little tale, so they kept humoring me, letting me talk. As long as I was talking, they were looking at me, not watching you and Mitch approach. . . . "

"Oh," said Tom. He unfolded his arms, scratched his head.

Brian shrugged. "I did what I could . . . in my own way."

Laura nodded. It was obvious to her that what Brian had done was brave and, from a tactical standpoint, pretty darn helpful. But Mitch spoke up before she could thank him.

"Okay, Tom, you got your answer. And that's *enough* rehashing of the pirate drama. Let's move on." Mitch swiveled his chair back to his keyboard and computer screen. "Come on, Brian, let's get back to work."

Laura didn't want to contradict Mitch, not while he was taking his captain's role so totally seriously, but she resolved to find Brian later and thank him privately.

"So, Mitch . . ." She stepped up to his chair and looked over his shoulder. "What else did you find out from the data on the island?"

Mitch scrolled down screen after screen of numbers and text. "The geothermal sensor was definitely made by Matsu Corporation. It was installed by Dr. Gensai, as I suspected. The first underground readings were taken about six weeks ago."

"Interesting," said Laura.

Tom sighed. "Except, none of that info is an earth-shattering breakthrough. We already knew Dr. Gensai was a geothermal scientist. We knew he worked for

Matsu Corporation. And we knew he visited the island from his wrinkled old chart."

"True," Mitch countered. "But I haven't gone though the sensor's entire memory yet."

Tom threw up his hands. "But you'll probably get nothing more than seismic readings, and that's a waste of time. What we need is a lead to help us find Emiko and her dad. What you should be concentrating on is Dr. Gensai's fried laptop computer." He pointed to the laptop they'd retrieved during the assault on Matsu Corporation's Mount Fuji facility. "That's the memory drive that's likely to have info we can use, like the location of Dragon Island."

"Stop it, Tom," Mitch replied. "Stop trying to take over. A ship can have only one captain if it's going to stay afloat, and I'm it! Like it or not, I'm setting the priorities. And that's all there is to it!"

A tense silence followed. Brian bowed his head like a kid upset by his parents' arguing. Tom seemed ready to scream. His arms were tightly folded and his face was red, but he held his tongue.

Laura, however, could no longer hold hers. "No," she told Mitch.

Mitch turned, surprised to find Laura the one speaking out against him. "No *what*?"

"You said that's all there is to it," she replied, "but

that's *not* all there is. You aren't being completely honest with your brother."

Brian's head snapped up. He met Laura's eyes. She knew Brian meant no harm in what he'd confided to her, but she'd had the same basic training that Tom and Mitch had experienced. Laura remembered what the sensei had taught her.

"To be R.O.N.I.N., you must be willing to endure the pain of unflinching honesty. . . ."

"You are impatient, Laura," Panther chided after a long session of sparring. "I see this in you. It is what fuels your temper . . . with yourself and others. I see this as a struggle you will have for years to come. But then . . . a girl of your age has a lot to learn, about the world, about herself. . . .

"If you continue to work hard, as you are now, I see you one day waking to a life where you will be the one in control—and not your emotions. . . ."

Laura had been stunned that Panther saw her and her shortcomings so clearly—yet saw a hopeful future for her too. And his words about honesty were something Mitch should have remembered from training too.

Now she faced Tom. "I have to tell you something, Tom. It's not very nice. But Mitch isn't being honest with you. He's beginning to doubt your visions. He's beginning to doubt that Dragon Island even exists."

Tom stood very still for a long moment, just staring at Laura. Then he shifted to meet his brother's eyes. Mitch refused to look at him.

"Is that true?" Tom asked.

Mitch nodded slowly.

Tom didn't utter another word. He simply turned in silence and strode off the bridge.

Brian tensed as Mitch wheeled on him. "Why did you tell her what I was thinking?"

Laura stepped up. "Don't pick on Brian. It's not his fault. He only told me the truth. You're not supposed to be afraid of the truth, Mitch."

"Except my brother didn't need to hear it, okay? You're to blame for that. How do you think you're helping anything by turning my brother against me?"

"Wake up, Mitch! Your little 'captain' role-playing game is what's alienating Tom. You want to hoard information so only you can make the decisions—but you have a crew here that has to live with those decisions."

Mitch opened his mouth to argue, but he suddenly remembered the pirate notation beside the first island on Dr. Gensai's map. Mitch had never shared that warning with anyone. He'd just made the command decision to dismiss it as ridiculous, but his friends had almost been killed because of that decision.

"You need to take a step back, Mitch," Laura continued. "You need to listen to the people 'beneath' you. And if you can't, well then . . . go ahead and be captain—without a crew!"

Laura turned and stalked to the door of the bridge. "Come on, Brian," she called. "Back on the beach you promised to help me with Emiko's memory crystal. I'd like your help now."

Brian remained seated. He glanced uncomfortably at Mitch.

"Go on," Mitch said in a defeated tone. "Go if you want to."

"I'll be back soon," Brian promised, rising. "Why don't you take a break and get a sandwich in the galley?"

"Just go, okay? Both of you!"

CHAPTER 10

With the bridge clear, Mitch closed his eyes to clear his mind, too.

Just because my crew's turned against me doesn't mean I have to get emotional about it. After all, the *Rakurai*'s fully automated. There's no reason I can't captain this ship without anyone else's help. . . .

With a deep breath, Mitch swiveled the tech chair back around to resume his analysis of the geothermal sensor data. But when he attempted to concentrate, the numbers and notations just seemed to melt together in a glowing green muddle.

In disgust, he rose and paced the bridge.

"How could they do it?" he murmured, feeling betrayed by Laura and Brian, even his own brother, who'd been challenging him nonstop from the day they had set foot on the ship.

"Why can't Tom just back me up like he does

during combat?" Mitch asked out loud.

"The very same question might be asked of you, young sir."

Mitch whipped around, expecting to see Mr. Chance in the doorway. But there was no one there. Had the voice of his guardian been in his mind?

Maybe I should talk to Mr. Chance about all this, he thought, pacing again. But he quickly dismissed the idea. It was Mr. Chance who'd assigned him the role of captain in the first place. Mitch didn't want to crash and burn, but who was he kidding? Given the mutiny of his crew, Mitch knew exactly what Mr. Chance would say. He would say he'd failed.

With a sigh, Mitch stopped pacing and realized he was standing right in front of the captain's chair. He thought of Tom again and the hurt look on his face when he'd left the bridge.

Mitch wanted to believe his brother's dreams were true visions, but Dr. Gensai's map had been well marked with notes of his Pacific journeys, and the words Dragon Island simply didn't appear on it!

Mitch shook his head. The farther along they got on this search, the more he needed to see some kind of proof that the island really existed. At this point, Tom's dreams weren't enough.

With a sigh of frustration, he collapsed into the

captain's chair. Beyond the bridge's front windshield, ugly storm clouds had formed along the horizon, and the *Rakurai* was plowing through a stretch of murky chop. The navigational coordinates were set for Dr. Gensai's next island, but Mitch began to wonder whether he was leading his crew in the wrong direction.

"You need to take a step back, Mitch." Laura's voice echoed back to him. "You need to listen to the people 'beneath' you. . . . "

For ten solid minutes, Mitch sat perfectly still in the captain's chair, thinking about what Laura had said. It wasn't easy for him to consider that he might be wrong, but a part of him knew that he had to get his crew back on his side.

And how am I going to do that?

Mitch's eye caught sight of the closed laptop computer, sitting on a map table a few feet away. He rose and walked over to it, finally deciding to try doing what Tom and Laura wanted. He was going to work on restoring Dr. Gensai's fried computer.

Pulling a small tool kit from his backpack, Mitch began to work. He tried everything he could think of to restore the computer.

He took the hardware apart and worked on the motherboard. He restored the drive's function and rebooted the software. He even reloaded the navigation programs and tried to access the lost memory from different programs, all without success.

Mitch ran a hand through his shaggy blond hair. Maybe I should just give up, he thought after a couple of hours. I've run out of options. About the only thing I haven't done is weigh the computer, take its pulse, and measure its blood pressure!

"Wait a second," he murmured. "Measure . . . " Suddenly Mitch decided to try something new.

After Laura left the bridge, she took Brian to the galley so he could get a bite to eat. Then she led him down to her cabin.

"Before we start on the memory crystal, Brian, I just

want to thank you," Laura said.

"Thank me? Why? I haven't done anything yet."

"Not for the crystal, for the distraction back on the island. You helped me by doing that."

Brian waved a dismissive hand.

"No, listen!" Laura urged. "When you drew the pirates' attention onto yourself, Mitch and Tom had surprise on their side when they attacked. That's a big tactical advantage, and you helped them get it. So thanks again."

Laura stepped closer. She knew Brian had a huge crush on her, and even though she didn't feel the same way, she wanted to thank him for his courage. But when she moved to kiss him on the cheek, Brian quickly stepped back.

"No, Laura," he said sharply. "You don't need to thank me. Let's just drop it, okay?"

"Oh? Um, okay . . . I understand," she said, but she really wasn't sure why he'd reacted the way he did.

Back on the beach, Brian had been dropping hint after hint that he liked her. And he'd always acted so arrogant, ready to compliment himself when someone else wasn't doing it for him. Yet now he didn't even want a little thank-you kiss for risking his neck with some bloodthirsty pirates? He actually seemed angry that she'd brought it up!

After an awkward silence, Brian explained, "I'm

just sorry that I couldn't fight them off for you. You know . . . like Tom and Mitch."

Now Laura understood—or at least she thought she did.

"You have nothing to be ashamed of," she quickly assured him. "Tom and Mitch have had"—she suddenly stopped herself before finishing—"they've had *special* training."

Laura knew not to mention what kind of training the brothers had been through. Brian didn't know about R.O.N.I.N., so she had to be careful.

"Yes, well . . . " Brian shifted impatiently on his feet. "Did you want to show me that memory crystal?"

Laura nodded and pulled the silver chain from around her neck. A small, pink, teardrop-shaped crystal emerged from beneath the neckline of her tank top. It was a memory drive exactly like the one Emiko had given to Laura back at the Matsu School.

"You know," said Laura, dangling the crystal in front of Brian, "the more I think about it, the more I think Emiko did what you said—she must have deliberately left this crystal behind for me to find, like a secret message."

"Perhaps she did."

"So this weird programming code that came right up—maybe it's really a secret message or something?"

"Show me," said Brian.

Laura grabbed her laptop off her cabin's dresser. Booting it up, she slipped the jewel of the necklace into the USB port. In a moment the code appeared on the screen.

Brian took the laptop over to Laura's bunk, sat down, and examined the programming.

"There's an EXE at the end of the file name," he said. "That means 'execute,' which tells me this is a command program to perform some task."

"I know that much," said Laura. "But what will it do once it's executed?"

Brian fiddled with the keyboard, sighed, and fiddled some more. "Sorry," he said, handing the small computer and necklace back to Laura. "I thought I might see a string of commands that would help, but this looks to me like it's set up to deactivate something very specific. I'll need a lot more time to decipher it."

Laura frowned. "If I plug this code into the right program, I'm sure *something* will happen."

"Yes, as I said, something will be deactivated," Brian repeated.

"But what is it supposed to deactivate?" Laura removed the crystal memory drive from the computer and handed the necklace back to Brian. "Here, why don't you take it? You can work more on it in your own cabin.

Let me know what you find out."

"Fine, but there's no guarantee—"

Just then a loud shout came from the bridge.

"Yeeeeeessss! I got it!" It was Mitch, yelling at the top of his lungs. "People! Do you hear me? I got it!"

CHAPTER 11

Everyone came running to the bridge: Laura, Brian, Tom, even Mr. Chance.

"I weighed Dr. Gensai's laptop," Mitch told them all. "The computer was nearly six ounces *heavier* than it's supposed to be, based on the make."

"What?" said Laura. "Why?"

"I took it apart again to find out," Mitch explained. "But this time I found a hidden compartment in the case itself. Inside was a second memory drive, not in any way connected to the first."

"Then Dr. Gensai's data isn't fried, after all!" Laura exclaimed. She glanced at Tom, but he just stood there with his arms folded.

"So, Mitch," he asked in a monotone, "what made you decide to work on the laptop?"

"I figured I owed it to you—and to Laura—for being such a jerk as captain," Mitch replied. "Look, I'm sorry

93

for the way I acted, okay? And I'm really sorry I doubted your visions, Tom."

Tom sighed. "The worst part is, bro . . . you've got me doubting them now too."

Laura stomped her foot. "What do you mean?"

"I mean, maybe Dragon Island is a figment of my imagination." Tom shrugged. "Maybe my dreams have nothing to do with reality."

For a full minute the bridge was silent. No one knew what to say. Finally Mr. Chance cleared his throat. All eyes turned to him.

"Perhaps you are both correct, young sirs," he said.

Tom and Mitch exchanged confused glances.

"How can we both be right?" asked Mitch.

"Yeah," said Tom. "Either Dragon Island exists or it doesn't."

"A tree falls but no one hears it," Mr. Chance replied. "Does it make a sound?"

"Huh?" said Laura and Tom.

"So, what if Dragon Island exists but doesn't exist?" Mitch asked.

"Excuse me?" said Laura.

"What if maps don't chart it?" Mitch suggested. "What if traditional satellites can't see it? But when you go there—"

"It *is* there!" Tom cried, suddenly feeling hopeful.

"But is it really possible to hide an island?"

"No," said Brian, waving his hand. "From a scientific standpoint, you'd have to have the ability to create constant cloud cover so a satellite could never pick it up. Who could do that?"

"Just because we've never heard of anyone manipulating weather doesn't mean it can't be done," Mitch pointed out.

Tom nodded. "There are things I never thought I could do that I can now. . . ." He exchanged glances with Mitch and Laura. "Who knows what's really possible?"

"It's all just speculation," said Brian.

Mr. Chance cleared his throat again. "There is a Japanese proverb that comes to mind at this juncture: 'Proof rather than argument.'"

"Mr. Chance is right," Mitch said. "I located Dr. Gensai's backup memory drive, but I haven't examined it yet. We need to take a look."

With everyone watching over Mitch's shoulder, he opened the data files. Within a few minutes, they located a digital map of the entire Pacific Ocean with strange-looking, snaky lines superimposed on it like vines on a wall.

"What are those?" Tom asked. "They're not longitude or latitude."

"I don't know," said Mitch.

"Maybe they're geothermal energy waves," Tom suggested.

"Or maybe just some personal cartographical markings that Dr. Gensai developed for his own purposes," said Mitch.

"Look," Laura exclaimed, pointing, "all of the lines seem to converge in one location."

Mitch nodded and read the coordinates aloud. "47 degrees 9 minutes 0 south 126 degrees 43 minutes 0 west in the southern Pacific Ocean."

Tom whistled. "That's hundreds of miles from our current position, in the biggest patch of empty ocean on Earth. I mean, there's, like, nothing out there . . . nothing at all."

Mitch put a hand on his brother's shoulder. "The perfect place for Dragon Island," he said confidently. He was now sure that Tom's island really existed, and was relieved to no longer doubt his brother.

"You think?" Tom asked hopefully.

"We will investigate," said Mitch, then glanced at Mr. Chance. "Proof rather than argument, right?" He grabbed a slip of paper and jotted down the coordinates.

"Brian, would you mind entering this data into the *Rakurai*'s navigational software?"

Brian tensed a moment.

"Brian?" Mitch turned to face his friend. "Do you feel okay? You look pale."

"I'm fine."

"Listen, why don't you take a break? I can handle this. No problem." Mitch began walking toward the tech chair, but Brian jumped in front of him.

"No!" he cried. "I'll do it!"

He took the slip of paper from Mitch's hand and began entering data into the ship's computer.

侍

"The sun's in the wrong place!" Mitch cried.

"Huh?" groaned Tom, opening his eyes. Sitting up in his bunk, he realized it was morning—early morning, not much past dawn. Mitch had just barged into his cabin.

Laura came running in after him, still dressed in her oversized New York Mets nightshirt. "Mitch, what's your problem?" she asked. "Why did you bang on my door?"

"We're heading south!" Mitch strode over to the large porthole and pointed outside. "The sun should be rising on the starboard side of the ship. But it's here, on the port side! We're off course!"

"But how could that be?" Laura asked. "The *Rakurai*'s computer is supposed to be infallible, isn't it? Wake up, Tom!" Laura cried. "We're in trouble!"

"No we're not." He yawned. "It's just human error. No big deal. Brian must have messed up with his typing, that's all. We can correct it easily enough, right, Mitch?"

Mitch took a breath and released it. "Right. Sure. I just . . . I just couldn't find Brian to ask him."

"What do you mean, you couldn't find Brian?" Laura asked. "He's not in his cabin?"

"No," said Mitch, "and he's not in the galley or on the bridge."

"Let's check the instruments," said Tom, now wide awake.

Mitch was already dressed, so he waited as Tom and Laura threw on some clothes. Then they all hurried up to the bridge to check the ship's computer.

Mitch quickly realized that Brian had programmed the navigational software with different coordinates than the ones from Dr. Gensai's digital map.

"This wasn't an accident," said Mitch. "These coordinates are very different from the ones I handed to Brian."

"That boy's been acting weird since the pirate attack," Laura commented. "What is his problem?"

No one had an answer for her as Mitch worked furiously on the computer.

"Just reprogram it," said Tom.

Mitch tried to, but he couldn't. "There's a security code in place on his changes. I can't get the computer to respond. For some reason, he's got us locked into a specific direction."

"So where *is* Brian?" Tom said. "We better search the ship."

CHAPTER 12

As Tom and Mitch began searching the decks, Laura ran back to double-check Brian's cabin. It was totally empty. His clothes were gone! She checked his closet and drawers. They were empty too. That's when she noticed something hanging from the edge of his mirror.

"Dog tags?" she whispered.

Laura read the tags. They belonged to someone in the U.S. military: Martin Masaharu Saito.

"Brian's father!"

Frantically, Laura searched for more clues left in the cabin. She spied a digital recorder on his pillow, right next to Emiko's memory crystal and a short note.

"'Dear Laura,'" she read aloud, "'Emiko's EXE file on this memory drive is set up to immediately deactivate one kind of coded avatar and then immediately launch another. That's all I can tell you because I ran out of time. Please play the recording and you'll understand.

Very sincerely yours, Brian Saito.'"

Draping the memory crystal back around her neck, Laura raced to the bridge with the digital recorder. Using the ship's intercom, she called Mitch, Tom, and Mr. Chance to come quickly to the bridge.

侍

"I'm so sorry," Brian's voice declared as Laura played back his digital recording. "But the pirates weren't pirates at all. The men who attacked us really worked for Julian Vane. They gave me my father's dog tags as proof that they're holding him prisoner. They've been tracking the *Rakurai* by satellite ever since we left the island, so I had no choice. I had to do as they demanded and reprogram the navigational software with the coordinates they gave me. I cannot tell you how sorry I am. How sad I am. All I can do now is warn you to watch your backs."

"Where *is* Brian?" Laura asked. "All his clothes and personal items were gone, except for the tags and this recording."

"One of the skiffs is missing," said Tom. "He must have taken it."

"We have to break his security code!" Mitch cried. "It's our only option."

"No," said Mr. Chance. "There is another. If Julian Vane desires a confrontation, then perhaps it is time we allowed it to happen—"

Suddenly the ship lurched abruptly, tipping on its side. Everyone was tossed to the deck as the crash alarms echoed throughout the ship.

The *Rakurai* had crashed into a massive reef just under the water's surface. The reef had clearly been the last stop for many other ships too. The wrecked old hulks stretched for at least a mile.

Beyond this debris was a tropical island. On it a massive tower rose up into the clouds. The steel construction appeared to be a giant broadcast antenna. Ringing the tower, hundreds of feet above the ground, was a five-story, saucer-shaped structure.

"What is that?" Laura wondered aloud.

"Looks like a supersize Seattle Space Needle," said Tom.

BOOM!

A cannon from one of the old, half-sunken ships suddenly began firing on them. The first attempt missed, but the second and third shook the ship.

BOOM! BOOM!

"Who's attacking us?" Laura cried.

"I don't know," said Mitch, "but we have to stop it or we're going to sink for sure!"

They all looked at one another.

"You stay with the ship," Mitch told his guardian. "Tom, Laura, and I will do what we can to take out whoever's firing on us."

侍

The briny scent of rotting seaweed was strong as Mitch exited the ship with his brother and Laura.

The reef in front of them was the surreal graveyard of old ships. There were oceangoing vessels from every era: pirate ships and ancient galleys; schooners and whaling ships from the nineteenth century. In the distance, a destroyer lay on its side, holed by a torpedo during World War II. Beside it lay a wrecked submarine.

"I don't believe it. . . . ," Mitch whispered.

"What?" said Laura.

"Where did all these ships come from? How long

have they been here? Why did they gather here?"

The trio stared at their surroundings, trying to make sense of what they were seeing, and trying to figure out the answers to Mitch's questions.

Suddenly Tom thought he saw something move among the rocks and he quickly scanned the area.

"Someone's watching us," he whispered ominously. But the noise of the cannon drowned out his words, so no one heard.

BOOM! BOOM!

"The cannon's firing from the east," said Mitch. "Let's move!"

The three climbed over the wreckage, jumping from rock to rock, over pools filled with squirming fish and dead sharks. A sucking noise came from a dying octopus flopping on this massive reef formed by the bones and shells from a billion dead sea creatures.

"Ugh! The air stinks!" Laura complained as they scrambled forward.

"This is like nothing I've ever seen before," said Mitch.

"It's unreal . . . unnatural," Tom murmured.

"Or supernatural," Laura said.

"What do you mean?" asked Mitch.

"I know exactly what Laura means," said Tom. "Don't you feel it too, bro? There's a kind of energy here. Waves of it, rolling through this place . . . "

Mitch exchanged glances with Laura. He didn't feel anything. And from the look on her face, he didn't think she felt anything either.

Mitch thought back to what Mr. Chance had said—about Dragon Island existing yet not existing. He wondered now if the same strange forces were in play for the island up ahead. Had some mystical energy created a mysterious fog, preventing ship after ship from seeing the danger ahead?

"It's like some force drew these ships to wreck here for years and years," said Tom.

"But why?" wondered Laura.

"I don't know," Tom replied. "Maybe to lure the ship's crews to serve here on this island?"

"Or their wrecked vessels to create a blockade," Mitch pointed out.

BOOM!

The more Mitch surveyed the reef and ships ringing the island, the more he realized that the surreal graveyard really did seem to serve as some kind of fortress for the island at its center, protecting it from direct assault.

With the *Rakurai* now under siege, Mitch, Tom, and Laura had no choice but to seek a way to fight beyond its bridge and decks.

They continued climbing over the rocks, reef, and

wreckage. Finally they reached the ship that was firing on the *Rakurai*—a rusted old Imperial Japanese Navy vessel that had run aground on the massive reef more than sixty years ago.

They moved toward the ship's forward gun turret, to take out whoever was firing the old cannon—but they never got there. A swarm of Black Lotus ninjas ambushed them.

The three teenagers had no chance to fight. Fishing nets were dropped on each of them. Then ninjas surrounded them. The men were dressed in black, their heads covered with black scarves, their hands holding drawn samurai swords.

"Surrender!" Mitch called to his brother and Laura. "Remember what Mr. Chance said!"

"Shut up!" one of the ninjas yelled, slamming Mitch in the shoulder with the heel of his sword.

Tom cursed and struggled against the web of nylon fishing net, desperate to defend his brother.

Mitch just gritted his teeth. "'If Julian Vane desires a confrontation,'" he loudly reminded Tom, "'then perhaps it is time we allowed it to happen.'"

"I said shut up!" the ninja repeated, striking Mitch again.

Tom cursed once more, but he stopped struggling. Both he and Laura realized that their captain was right.

The smartest thing they could do now was surrender, and that's exactly what they did.

Steeling themselves for the face-off to come, Mitch, Tom, and Laura allowed themselves to be dragged as prisoners toward the massive broadcast tower on the island beyond.

DYLAN SPROUSE AND COLE SPROUSE ARE TWO OF HOLLYWOOD'S MOST EMINENT RISING STARS.

Dylan and Cole were born in Arezzo, Italy, and currently reside in Los Angeles, California. Named for the jazz singer and pianist Nat King Cole, Cole's list of favorites includes math, the color blue, and animals. He also enjoys video games and all types of sports, including motocross, snowboarding, and surfing. Dylan, named after the poet Dylan Thomas, is very close to his brother and also has a great love of animals and video games. He enjoys science, the Los Angeles Lakers, and the color orange. He's a sports enthusiast and especially loves motocross, snowboarding, surfing, and basketball.

Cole and Dylan made their acting debuts on the big screen in *Big Daddy*, opposite Adam Sandler. Both also starred in *The Astronaut's Wife*, *Master of Disguise*, and *Eight Crazy Nights*. On television Cole and Dylan established themselves in the critically acclaimed ABC comedy series *Grace Under Fire* and eventually went on to star in NBC's *Friends* as David Schwimmer's son, Ben Geller.

Dylan and Cole currently star as the introspective Cody Martin and the mischievous Zack Martin, respectively, in the Disney Channel's amazingly successful sitcom *The Suite Life of Zack and Cody*, playing separate roles for the first time. Ranked number one in its time slot against all basic cable shows, *The Suite Life* is now one of the Disney Channel's top shows and is rapidly gaining worldwide success.

In September 2005 the Sprouses partnered with Dualstar Entertainment Group to launch the *Sprouse Bros.* brand, the only young men's lifestyle brand designed by boys for boys. The brand includes *Sprouse Bros. 47 R.O.N.I.N.*, an apparel collection, an online fan club, mobile content, a DVD series in development, and lots more in the works!

SPROUSE
BROS

CHECK OUT

sprousebros.com

FOR GOOD TIMES, SWEET CONTESTS AND THE LATEST ON DYLAN, COLE AND THE SPROUSE BROS BRAND!